A Louis Louis Book

Louis finds a new home

For Margaret my Mum

A Louis Louis book

published by

wee dug books 2011

Author
Gillian Muir

Illustrator
Delphine Frantzen

Dog
Louis

A little dog sat tied to a post.
He was very sad.
The big dogs barked.

His coat was overgrown
and he looked like a
little brown bear.
He sat and he waited.

They came to look at another dog
but then they saw him.

The boy knelt down to pat him.

The dog cuddled in close to the boy
and wagged his little brown tail.

"This is the one. Can we take him home?"

The lady in the office said first they
should take him for a walk.

The little dog behaved very well.

Back in the office the lady asked
them lots of questions.

"Do you have any other pets?"
"Have you ever had a pet dog?"
"Do you have a garden?"

Now and again the little dog scratched his sore ears and itched his overgrown coat.

"Yes we have a cat called Buzz."
"Yes we have had a pet dog."
"Yes we have a garden with trees and plenty of sticks!"
"Can we take him home now?"

Forms were filled out and checks
were made.
"Now you can take him to his new
home," said the lady.
The little brown dog leapt up
into the car.

"One last question!" she shouted.
"Will you keep his old name?"
"No," said the boy.
"We will call him Louis!"

Louis sat on the front seat looking
straight ahead.
Behind him he left the dog shelter

They drove out of the city,
through the forest,
up the cobbled road
to his new home.

Louis slowly walked
through the doorway.

He looked all around
but didn't know
where he was.

They led him into the kitchen and
opened the back door to the garden.

Louis sat on the top step
and looked out.

They had everything
ready for Louis.
A new bed with
a comfy blanket.
One bowl for food
and one for water.
Dog food and
dog treats.
A box of toys
with interesting
things in it.
A tartan collar
with a name tag on
it in the shape of a bone.

The girl took one look at Louis and said, "He is adorable!"

They kicked the ball and
Louis chased it.
He ran and ran.
Buzz their cat jumped
over the gate to see
what all the fuss was about.

When he first arrived
Louis cried at night.
It was a sad lonely howl.
They spoke softly to him
and stroked his fluffy head.
He looked up at them.

It was all very confusing
for little Louis.

Even Buzz the cat
looked concerned.

He jumped down
from the window sill
and curled up
beside Louis.

It was as if he was telling him,
"You will be safe here."

A few days later they took Louis to see a vet.
She put him up on a table for a check over.
She looked at his eyes,
in his ears
and heard his heart beat.
Opened his mouth,
checked his teeth
and put him on
scales to be weighed.

He did not like it one bit!

Louis jumped off the table and stood at the door.
He looked frightened and very cross.
The boy picked him up, held him close and told him
that everything was going to be fine.

The vet gave them
eye drops,
ear drops
and cream
for sore skin.
Louis was very
pleased to leave
and go back
to his new home.

TOILETTAGE ERIX

Next stop was to get Louis a hair cut.
When they arrived some dogs
already had new hair-dos.
A large poodle had a pompom
tail and pompom legs,
a brown grumpy dog had
a newly trimmed beard which
made him look very important
and a little dog was very white
indeed and looked like she was
made of candy floss.

Louis looked around and decide
a hair cut was NOT for him!

Louis was carefully lifted on to the table.

Then after the buzz buzz buzzing
of the clippers.
And the snip snip snipping
of the scissors.
The little brown furry dog was turned
into...

A handsome cocker spaniel!

Louis stood tall and proud.
His coat was velvet brown.
He wagged his little brown tail.

Everything was new to him.
The girl blew bubbles in the garden
and he jumped up as high as the sky to catch them.
He was starting to have fun.

They took him out and about.
They stopped to look at
the musical fountain.
The water
came whooshing
out of the
different instruments.
It always made them smile.

Louis could not believe his little brown eyes.

At the park there were
even more things to discover.
Louis saw ducks for the first time.
What a noise they were making.
He wanted to investigate but
they kept him on a very short lead!

Then he spotted a turtle
sitting on a log
basking in the sun.

Louis had been a city dog
and now he wanted to
see it all.

Louis trotted around the park
with his head held high.
He saw a statue of a deer.
He started to bark at it.
People smiled at this
curious little dog.

He stopped suddenly when
he heard a strange noise.
They took him over to the pond
to see a frog sitting on a lily pad.
"RIBBIT RIBBIT RIBBIT."

He spent hours in the garden with the children.
"Louis Louis!" they called.
He bounded over to them.
They played and played.
When they stopped to rest
he would keep guard.

After a long day
and a cool bowl of water
with ice cubes
Louis would finally allow himself to lie down and relax

Sometimes at the end of the day
they would look out and see Louis sitting
like a little statue staring up to the sky.

"It's a big world out there Louis," they said.
"It's time to explore!"

Follow the adventures of Louis
as he travels the world...